This edition published by Parragon Books Ltd in 2016 and distributed by

Parragon Inc.
440 Park Avenue South, 13th Floor
New York, NY 10016
www.parragon.com

Written by Margaret Wise Brown
Illustrated by Antoine Corbineau

ISBN 978-1-4748-5742-0

Printed in China

# The
# DIGGERS

# PaRRagon

Bath • New York • Cologne • Melbourne • Delhi
Hong Kong • Shenzhen • Singapore

# DIG DIG DIG

A mole was digging a hole.

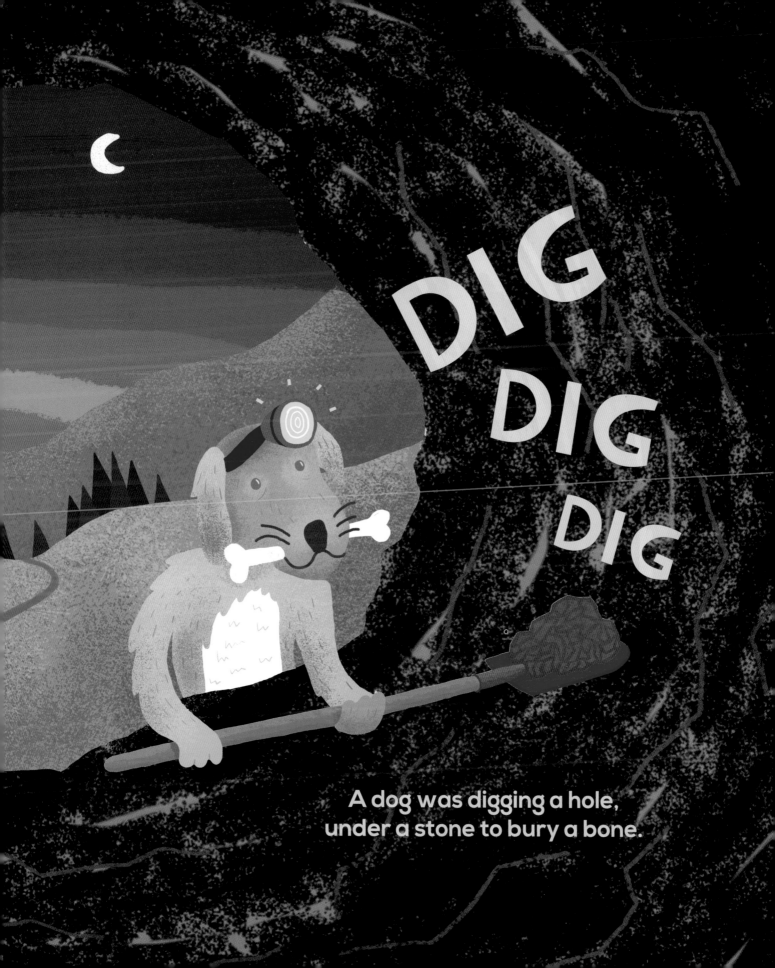

DIG DIG DIG

A dog was digging a hole,
under a stone to bury a bone.

DIG DIG

DIG

A worm was digging a hole.

He swallowed the ground,

as he wiggled around,

and ate his way toward home.

DIG DIG DIG

A rabbit was digging a hole.

Next to a mouse,
who was digging a house,

in a little warm hole
in the ground.

DIG

DIG

# DIG

A pirate was digging a hole.

A hole in the sand
to bury his gold,

and the diamonds
and rubies he stole.

# DIG DIG DIG

In the city, a man was digging a hole.

Monday he dug,

Tuesday he dug,

And then came the big digger,
    made by a man to dig deeper and bigger.

To scoop up stones,
and find dinosaur bones,
and cavemen's homes,
and buried gnomes.

**DIG**
**DIG**
**DIG**

The shovel dug its way.

Night after night,

day after day,

it dug.

And a great big hole ran under the city,
under a river,
and into the bright green country.

A man put a
train in the hole.

And the train ran under the street.
Under the city, under the river, until

it popped out of
the hole into bright
green country.

It went past ducks and geese,
and donkeys and cows,
and sheep and fields
of galloping horses.

Until it came to a mountain

and couldn't get over

and couldn't get through

and couldn't get around.

And so it had to stop.
But not forever.

For down the track came another train.
And on the last car rode the great digger.

Under the mountain it dug away,
night after night, day after day.

Until, with one last bite
it came to daylight on the
other side of the mountain.

And soon the train came through the mountain and onto the great green plain beyond.

And on went the train,
on and on,
down its long steel track.

And the smoke trailed back,
and back,
and back.